PEST CONTROL

CAVAN SCOTT

Badger
LEARNING

Pest Control ISBN 978-1-78147-797-7

Text © Cavan Scott 2014
Complete work © Badger Publishing Limited 2014

Publisher: Susan Ross
Senior Editor: Danny Pearson
Publishing Assistant: Claire Morgan
Copyeditor: Cheryl Lanyon
Designer: Bigtop Design Ltd

2 4 6 8 10 9 7 5 3 1

CHAPTER 1

FRESH MEAT

Alice White felt as if everyone knew what she was planning as soon as she stepped through the supermarket doors. She headed past the magazines, past the flowers, past the thick-necked security guard who glared at her from beneath a heavy brow.

She nearly lost her nerve there and then. Nearly turned around and walked back out. But then what would Dad do?

She kept her head down, carefully avoiding everyone's gaze. Down the first aisle, dodging the old woman who was pushing a trolley at a snail's pace. Around the toddler having a tantrum on the floor.

Alice's heart was thudding in her chest, so loudly she was sure everyone could hear it. One hand was shoved in her coat pocket, the other gripping the strap of her school bag as if someone was about to rip it from her shoulder.

She hurried past the bakery and jams, and on to the fresh meat chiller. She could do this. She would have to. Do it for Dad.

What other choice did she have?

She reached the chiller cabinets and peered inside. Whole chickens. Legs of lamb. Packs of mince. Now she was here she didn't know what she should get – what he needed.

Her hand shook as she tried to slide the cabinet lid open. It wouldn't budge. Another chance to give up and make her escape. Perhaps someone was trying to tell her something.

An arm crossed in front of her. "Here, love. Let me help."

Alice looked up. A woman in her fifties smiled back as she yanked the chiller open. "A devil to open, that one. Always has been. They should do something about it."

"Thanks," Alice mumbled and turned back to the food in the cabinet. The woman continued on her way, happy to have performed her good deed of the day.

Alice felt guiltier than ever.

She looked back into the chiller and spotted the steaks at the bottom. Which should she take? Braising steak? Sirloin? Rib eye? There were too many to choose from. What if she chose the wrong one? Dad would be angry and there was no telling what he would do. Not any more.

Get a grip on yourself, Alice thought. *Pick one and get out. What are you waiting for?*

She reached deep into the cabinet, almost having to bend double to reach the bottom.

The biggest. That's what he'd want. The juiciest.

Her fingers found a pack of bloody rump steak. Without hesitating, Alice snatched it up and slipped the meat into her open bag. She walked away without shutting the cabinet.

Just get out, she told herself, *as quickly as you can. Don't run, though. Never run. If you run they wonder what you've done. Running draws attention. Running gets you caught.*

Alice strode down the central aisle, head down. There was a long queue for the checkout at the front of the store. Good. She could use it as a shield. Nip behind it, out of sight of the checkout girl.

She scanned the queue, groaning when she noticed the woman who'd helped her with the chiller cabinet.

Please don't talk to me, Alice willed her. *Please. Please. Please.*

It was as if the woman heard her thoughts. She turned and flashed her a smile.

"Not get what you wanted, love?"

"N-no," Alice stuttered as she rushed by. "Doesn't matter. I can come back."

The woman didn't take the hint. "You should ask the manager. They might have some out back."

Alice didn't reply. She was sure that she'd blown it, that the security guard's meaty hand was going to crash down on her shoulder any second. What would happen to Dad then? Who would find him?

What would they find?

The exit was in her sights now. She wanted to race for the doors. Anything to get out of the harsh glow of the store's strip lighting, away from suspicious eyes.

On the other side of the tills, the security guard turned to look at her. This was it. He knew. They all did. Alice started sprinting, almost bashing into the doors before they had a chance to open.

She didn't know if the security guard was chasing her. She didn't stop to see. She barrelled out of the shop, nearly crashing into a mother struggling with a buggy.

"Sorry," Alice spluttered, ignoring the glare from the young mum. She ran across the car park and out onto the high street, never looking back.

She just needed to get home, back to Dad. Back to the man who had made her a thief.

CHAPTER 2

HOME SAFE

Alice could hardly breathe by the time she got home. She had never run so fast, dodging down side streets, using every short-cut she knew.

She'd imagined footsteps chasing after her, but there was no one there when she finally glanced over her shoulder. No angry security guards. No police.

She'd got away with it, even though the guilt was already gnawing away at her guts. She never wanted to go through that again, but what choice did she have? Was this how it was going to be from now on? Until Dad started earning again?

If Dad ever started earning again.

She scrambled for her keys at the bottom of her bag, the polystyrene tray brushing against her hand. Reminding her of what she'd done. What she had become.

You do what you need to do, that was what Dad always used to tell her after Mum had gone. *That's how we'll get through this,* he said the first time they sat and ate a meal on their own, just the two of them. *We'll look after each other. Just you and me. That's all we need.*

The door opened and she slipped inside. The hallway inside was dark, all the curtains in the house closed. The world shut out.

The place was boiling, though, the heating on full blast. Like the hothouse at the zoo.

"Dad, I'm back," she called out, shrugging off her bag and hanging her coat on the end of the bannister. There was no answer from upstairs.

"I've got your tea."

Alice grabbed the pack of meat from the bag and walked through to the kitchen. At least she felt safe now. No one could hurt her while she was at home.

She busied herself, trying to act as if all this was normal. Choosing one of the yellow plates from the cupboard, the one with the blue rim. They were Dad's favourites, always had been.

She grabbed a small knife, splitting open the pack's clear plastic. She grabbed the steak and transferred it to the plate as quickly as possible. The feel of the meat between her fingers made her stomach lurch. The soft, spongy flesh. The drops of blood splattering across the worktop.

She almost licked the juices from her fingertips before stopping herself. Gross! She turned on the cold tap and thrust her hand beneath the water, watching the red stuff swirl down the plughole.

There was a noise from above. A thud. Dad moving around his room, getting impatient. He needed his lunch. Needed the meat.

The plate scraped as she picked it up from the worktop. She paused at the kitchen door.

"You can do this," Alice told herself. "After the supermarket, this shouldn't be a problem. He's just your dad."

The bangs continued upstairs. He was hungry.

He was always hungry these days.

Alice started up the stairs, the steps creaking beneath her feet. Across the landing towards his bedroom door. She went to knock on the wood, hesitating once again.

Pull yourself together, she thought. *It will be over in a minute.*

Until tomorrow.

She rapped on the door. "Dad? It's me. It's Alice."

Her dad groaned softly on the other side of the wood.

"I'm coming in," she said. "Can you move away from the door?"

She listened, hearing his feet scrape on the carpet. Then, when she was sure he'd moved to the other side of the room, she pulled a key from her jeans pocket. It slipped into the lock and turned easily.

Alice took a deep breath and pushed the door open.

The room was mostly empty, save for the broken furniture scattered across the floor. Where was he? Where was her dad?

Her eyes flicked to the ceiling. There he was, sitting in the corner like a spider. He was staring at her with hungry, black eyes. All six of them.

That was new. He'd only had four when she'd left.

"C-come down from there," she said, trying to keep her voice steady. "I've got you something to eat."

Dad dropped, flipping over in mid-air to land on all-fours on the filthy carpet. At least that was normal. Two arms and two legs. As it should be.

He scampered towards her on his hands and knees. She couldn't remember the last time she'd seen him standing upright.

"Gimme," he ordered. "Gimme meat."

CHAPTER 3

DAD

As quickly as she could, she dropped the plate onto the bedside cabinet. It was one of the only pieces of furniture he hadn't smashed. Mum had always loved that old oak cabinet with its fancy gold handles. Alice's dad slammed into it in his haste, knocking the set of drawers roughly against the wall.

He scooped the steak up in clawed hands, cramming it into his mouth. It was as if she disappeared while he was eating. All he cared about was the meat. Alice knew she should leave but couldn't stop herself watching. Her dad tore a chunk off the steak with his teeth, chewing loudly. The blood dribbled down his chin, catching on the stubble.

He was getting worse. As he gobbled the meat, Alice thought back to the first day of this nightmare. She remembered it so clearly. Dad was a pest controller, sent to clear rats and insects out of people's houses. He always moaned when he came home, complaining about all the filth and the smell. This day was different. This day he was in pain.

He moved straight to the sink, running his hand under the cold water. A blister covered the length of his thumb. He'd been scratched exterminating the biggest bugs he'd ever seen. As big as your head, he joked. Dad was always joking, making up stories. This time his voice quavered when he spoke. What he'd seen had scared him. The wound looked painful. A sac of yellow pus surrounded by angry, red skin. Alice said he should go to the doctor's, but Dad tried to laugh it off.

"It's nothing, love. Just a scratch."

It didn't look like nothing to her.

Dad opened the medicine cabinet and slapped some antiseptic cream on the blister.

"We look after each other, remember," he said as he wrapped a bandage around the wound. "We don't need anyone else. The Whites against the world, eh?"

When Alice nodded he gave her a cheery thumbs up – the bandage was already turning yellow where the poison was seeping through.

She shouldn't have listened to him. She should have made him go to the health centre.

The next day he called in sick. He lay on the sofa, watching old quiz shows on Challenge TV. He couldn't stop coughing, horrible, hacking coughs that sounded full of muck. Alice didn't go to school. He wasn't happy about that but she insisted on staying home to look after him. It was the end of the week anyway. No one would miss her. She just wanted to get her dad well again.

But he didn't get better. She watched him get worse over the weekend. His skin looked waxy and seemed too tight across his bones. The cough got worse, too. Dad started wheezing and then making an even stranger noise. Like a clicking at the back of his throat. Like the chirrup of an insect.

She came back from school two days later to find him scrubbing his leg with a brush. His eyes were wild and bloodshot, almost as red as the patch of raw skin where he'd rubbed too hard.

His legs were covered in coarse, black hairs. They were tiny and curved like knives. They were sprouting on his hands and arms too. Even his cheeks.

"Nothing to worry about," he growled, his voice strained as if in pain. "Just feeling a little run down. Body playing up. Need to rest." He paused, fixing her with his bloodshot eyes. "Need to eat."

So she started to make tea, getting sausages out of the fridge. She turned to get a frying pan, only to find him shoving the raw sausages into his mouth.

By the end of the week he'd made her lock him into his bedroom. Said he needed to be alone. She would have to get the food to feed them both. But the money soon ran out and Dad couldn't remember the PIN number for his cash card.

He couldn't even remember her name.

She wanted to get help, but he wouldn't hear of it. He would get better. She just had to trust him.

Her dad. The monster. The man with six eyes who could walk on ceilings. Like a bug.

She couldn't trust him any more. Not when he was like this.

It was now or never.

"Dad," she said. "I think I should tell someone at school."

His head snapped up. "No," he hissed. "No school. You stay here. With me."

Tears blurred her vision. "I can't, Dad. This is too much. I'm scared. Really, really scared."

"NO!" he shouted, swiping at the plate with his arm. It flew through the air, smashing on the far wall. "You stay here. With me."

Downstairs, the doorbell rang in the hall. Alice glanced over her shoulder and then back at her dad. Now what was she supposed to do?

"Don't answer it," Dad commanded, his thin lips drawing back to reveal sharp teeth. "Stay here with me."

She shook her head. Not this time.

"It could be important," she said, going to leave. This could be the help they needed. "I've got to go."

"Stay with me," her dad roared and leaped towards her.

CHAPTER 4

HELP COMES TO CALL

Alice screamed as her dad grabbed at her, fingers closing tight around her arm. No, not fingers – claws. She pulled away, dragging her arm from his grip.

Pain shot up her arm. She cried out, stumbling back against the wall. She looked down at her arm. An ugly scratch ran from her wrist to her elbow. It wasn't deep, but it already stung dreadfully.

Alice's dad stumbled back, staring at her arm.

"I'm sorry," he mumbled. "Sorry, sorry, sorry."

He looked so pathetic, cringing against the remains of his bed. Holding her arm, Alice backed quickly out of the room and slammed the door.

The scratch burned beneath her skin. Enough was enough. She'd played by his rules ever since the accident, but no more.

The doorbell rang again, followed by a sharp rap against the door.

Alice ran down the stairs, nearly slipping as she reached the bottom step. She crossed over to the door and pulled it open.

A familiar face stood on the other side. A tall man with a bald head and a broad smile. One of Dad's workmates, Steve.

His grin faded as he took in how Alice looked.

"You OK, pet?" he asked, worry lines creasing his forehead. "I just popped around to see your dad."

She nodded, hiding her throbbing arm behind her back.

"Y-yeah, I'm fine," she said as brightly as she could. "Sorry. Just been…" she searched for the right lie, "just been doing my homework. Algebra. Hate it."

Steve laughed. "Don't blame you. Was always rubbish at Maths, me. All those numbers." He pulled a face as if he'd smelled something horrible, before breaking into a smile. "Still, someone's got to do it. So, is your dad OK?"

Steve peered over her shoulder into the gloomy hallway.

Alice pulled the door closer to her, closing the gap.

"Yeah, he's fine," she said, trying a weak smile.

"He's getting better, then?"

She nodded, biting her lip.

"That's good, then," Steve said. "The lads have been worried about him at work. Getting the flu like that."

"That's nice," she said, wishing Steve would go away. This was crazy. A minute ago she was all for asking for help, but now someone was here she didn't know what to do. She could hear her dad's words ringing in her ears.

We look after each other. The Whites against the world.

Steve didn't take the hint. "Boss is getting a little funny, though. Says Bob needs to send in a doctor's note. Your dad, I mean. Has he been to see the doc?"

"Oh yeah," Alice said, the lies coming thick and fast now. "He, er, went last week. Told him to rest."

"And he got a note?"

"Think so, yeah."

"I could take it into work, then," Steve offered. "Help out, like. If you want me to?"

Alice wanted to slam the door in his face.

"I'm not sure where it is," she said, wondering how long she could keep this up.

"I could help you search for it," said Steve, looking like he was about to barge through the door.

"No!" Alice said, with a little too much force. Steve looked taken aback. Suspicious. She made herself laugh. "It's a mess in here and Dad's asleep. Tell you what, I'll find it and bring it round to you later. Does that sound OK?"

Steve didn't look convinced. "Well, I guess so…"

Upstairs, a door opened. Her mouth went dry. Alice glanced up towards the landing as a shadow scuttled towards the bathroom. No! She hadn't locked the door. Dad had been clear on that, back when he was making sense.

Always lock the door, Alice. From the outside. No matter what I say, don't let me out.

"What was that?" Steve asked, trying to peer around the door.

"The cat," Alice replied quickly. "He's got out of my bedroom."

"Didn't know you had one."

Alice nodded. "I'd better catch him before he wakes Dad. Thanks for calling around. I'll pop by with that note later."

"Alice, wait –"

She shut the door in Steve's face and raced upstairs.

There was the sound of breaking glass. The bathroom! Alice tore along the landing, but it was too late. The bathroom window was smashed, the wooden frame hanging loose from the wall.

Frantically, she looked out of the gap it had left but there was nothing in the garden.

And then, two houses down, something leaped over a fence. Something big, a large, black shell glinting in the afternoon sun.

She ran back to Dad's bedroom. This time it really was empty, except for a pile of shredded clothes by the door.

No. Not just clothes. Shredded skin, tangled in her dad's shirt and jeans.

She wanted to be sick. She wanted to run downstairs and call after Steve, ask him to help find her dad. But she knew that was impossible. Dad was different now. He'd changed into… something. Something with a glossy, black shell that could smash through windows and leap fences.

And it was up to her to find him.

CHAPTER 5

THE CHASE

Alice grabbed her keys and rushed out of the front door. Steve was standing in the street, talking urgently into his mobile phone.

"Alice, pet?" he called after her as she raced down the road. "What's wrong? What happened?"

She didn't answer. No time for busybodies, even if they meant well. There was a lane at the end of the road, next to the shabby old pillar box. She could cut behind the houses – not that she had a clue what she would do when she caught up with her dad.

If he still was her dad.

The light was already fading as Alice charged into the narrow alleyway, evening drawing in. Nearby she heard the thud of something large hitting the floor, followed by the frenzied yapping of a small dog. Her arm ached as she bolted down the lane, following the sounds. The dog's barking got more and more frantic, before it stopped abruptly. Too abruptly. The thought of what must have happened made her feel sick.

There was more clattering up ahead. She turned a corner, finding herself in a narrow walkway. A garden gate was hanging open at the far end. Two wheelie bins were lying across the path, rubbish strewn across the floor. Crisp packets fluttered in the breeze, a tin can rolled towards her. She stopped it with her foot.

This could only just have happened. He must be nearby.

Something moved in the garden beyond the gate. Something dark and squat.

"Dad?"

With a hiss it scuttled out of the gate, running straight towards her.

Clack, clack, clack, clack.

It was a bug the size of a man – and not just any man. Alice screamed, throwing herself back, but the insect didn't attack her. It scurried past, its black shell gleaming and long antennae twitching in the cool air. The creature shot out of the lane, clambering up a brick wall as it turned the corner. Trying to escape. Trying to get away from her.

She couldn't let it go.

"Wait, please!"

Alice ran after the insect, calling her dad's name. He didn't stop. Could he still understand English? Did he even know who she was?

The lane opened out onto a new estate. The bug scampered across the road, right into the path of a large car. The people-carrier's horn blared, the driver slamming on the brakes. It was as if time slowed down. Alice screamed as the car swerved to the left, headlights picking out red markings on the giant insect's back. She was sure that her dad's transformed body was going to be crushed to a pulp beneath the thundering wheels.

The car screeched to a halt, mounting the curb, but there was no dull thud as front bumper met hard shell. Her dad had made it! Alice ran onto the road. He was nowhere to be seen.

She passed in front of the car, the driver already out of his door.

"Did you see that?" he called over to her. "What was that thing?"

She didn't answer. He wouldn't believe her if she told him, anyway. Ahead was another lane, this time leading down to the cycle path. Could Dad have scampered down there, or had he headed around the back of the houses to the left? She stood for a second, not knowing which way to turn, scratching at her arm.

As the driver checked his front wheels, Alice made her decision. The cycle path. She didn't know how she knew, but she was certain that her dad had gone that way. She could feel it in her guts.

*

The bike path ran alongside a dual carriageway. Lorries thundered past, their headlights flashing as Alice darted across the lanes. She shivered. It was getting dark and cold. She hugged her injured arm to her, looking from left to right.

No sign of Dad. Perhaps she'd been wrong. Maybe he hadn't come this way at all.

Behind her something hissed. She span around, finding herself face-to-face with the giant bug.

"D-Dad?" she stammered, backing away. "It is you, isn't it?"

The insect made a clicking noise and cocked its head in the very same way her dad had looked at her in his bedroom.

She took a step forwards, trembling from head to foot.

It's just Dad, she told herself. *Just the man who picked you up when you grazed your knee as a kid, made everything better with a hug. The same man.*

Except it wasn't. That man hadn't had huge, clacking jaws and antennae that swept through the air in front of her. That man didn't hiss and chatter. That man wasn't a monster.

"It's OK," Alice said. "We can sort this. Just the two of us. The Whites against the world."

As she spoke, Alice raked at her arm. The bug's head jerked towards her hand. She looked down at her shaking fingers. Blood was caked beneath her fingernails. The insect hissed louder than ever, thick mucus spraying from its gaping jaws.

It could smell her blood, the same thick, coppery scent that filled her nostrils.

Steaks from the supermarket were no longer enough. The bug that used to be her father craved fresher meat.

CHAPTER 6

CORNERED

The insect bounded forwards. Alice let out a cry, throwing herself to the side and rolling on the floor. The bug crashed into the bushes that separated the bike path from the dual carriageway. It flailed around, trying to pull its six strong legs from the tangled branches.

This was her chance. She didn't think about which way to run. She just knew she needed to get away.

Alice pounded along the bike path, running away from the hissing creature. The traffic roared past as she came to a fork in the path. She could either continue down beneath a dark canopy of trees, or up across the bridge that led to the shopping centre on the other side of the road. The lights of a clothes store shone out like a beacon. That's where she'd head. That's where she'd be safe from that thing.

That's where she'd find help.

Her dad's words echoed through her head as she started to climb the metal stairs two steps at a time.

We don't need anyone, Alice.

We look after each other.

The Whites against the world.

Yeah, well that was before he wanted to eat her.

The bug reached the bottom of the steps. She glanced over her shoulder to see it scuttling up behind her. Big mistake. Her foot caught under the last step and she tripped, crashing forwards.

Pain shot up her leg as her ankle twisted, but that was nothing compared to the shock of her chin hitting the floor. Her teeth cracked together and it was as if a firework went off inside her head. Stars burst across her vision and for a moment Alice had no idea where or who she was.

Then she heard legs on the stairs. Lots of legs.

Clack, clack, clack, clack.

She pushed herself up, trying to run, but her ankle gave out beneath her. She crashed to the floor of the bridge again, dragging herself along now, her nails scraping on the cold metal.

The creature was behind her. That was all she needed to ignore the pain, that and the lights from the stores on the other side of the road.

Alice snatched for the metal handrail. Hauling herself up, she limped forwards. She knew she couldn't move quickly enough, knew that she would never escape, but she had to try.

Claws scrabbled against metal and Alice stumbled again. It was useless. She slammed down onto the floor, twisting around as the insect loomed over her. Its mandibles clicked together as she tried to crawl away on her back, her head cracking painfully against the bridge railings.

More fireworks. More stars.

This was it. No way out. She was going to die and there was nothing anyone could do about it. There was no one who could help after all.

"Come on then," she screamed at the thing that used to be her dad. "What are you waiting for?"

The insect's head twitched and it backed away from her slightly. Was it getting ready to pounce, or was this something else?

Alice grabbed hold of one of the railings and pulled herself into a sitting position. Her useless leg was stretched in front of her, her arm burning hot, and yet the bug hesitated. Had it recognised her? Did it know who she was?

"D-dad?" she said, praying that her father was still in there somewhere.

The bug's antennae quivered at the sound of the name. Yes. It was him.

Tears tumbled down her cheeks. "Daddy, I'm scared…"

The insect raised a front leg, as if it wanted to reach out to her. Like Dad always used to. Brushing a tear away from her cheek. Pulling her in for a hug. Holding her close.

The memory made the tears flow freely.

Whatever had happened to him, he was still her dad.

"Get away from her!"

The yell came from the steps. Steve was standing at the end of the bridge, horror written over his face. Her dad hissed, scuttling back.

"No!" Alice called out, throwing up a hand. "You don't understand."

"Alice, run! Get out of here!"

"Steve, please!"

He sprinted towards them, waving his arms in the air, trying to shoo what he thought was a monster away.

"Get away! Get away from her!"

Alice looked back at the bug and their eyes locked – but there was no recognition any more. Only fear. Rage.

Hunger.

The giant insect drew back, spit flicking from its jaws. Alice screamed, pressing herself into the rails as it leaped forwards. She screwed her eyes up tight, throwing her hands over her face. She imagined the claws slicing across her arms, those jaws closing tight.

Somewhere far away Steve called her name but all she could hear was the bug's angry hiss. It drowned everything out, consuming her entire world – and passed over her head.

Alice opened her eyes, craning her neck as the bug disappeared over the side of the railing. It had overshot, tumbling from the bridge. She tried to turn, but Steve was there now, grabbing her shoulders.

"Alice, are you OK? Did it hurt you?"

She fought against him, wanting to see.

The blare of a truck's horn cut through the night, followed by the screech of brakes – and a dull, sickening thud.

Alice screamed her dad's name.

EPILOGUE

Alice lay on the bed in the back of the ambulance. The paramedic was talking to her but she couldn't focus on the words. The last few moments on the bridge kept replaying in her mind, over and over again.

Steve's shout.

The bug jumping.

Flying over her head.

The crunch on the road below.

Steve said she had been lucky, the creature overshooting like that. Falling to its death.

Was that what had happened? Had the monster taken over at the last moment? The hunger driving him wild?

Or had her dad known what he was doing? Had he made sure that he could never hurt her again?

The ambulance doors slammed shut and the driver started the engine. The bed rocked gently as they pulled off the bike path and onto the road.

The paramedic appeared above her, checking the drip he'd connected to her arm.

We'll be at the hospital soon," he promised. "Is there anyone we can call for you?"

Alice shook her head and looked away, gazing at the wall.

No one to call. No one to help.

She was on her own.

Alice White against the world.

The paramedic returned to his seat and started filling out a bunch of forms as the driver fired up the siren.

Soon be at the hospital.

Alice scratched at her arm. They had covered the scratch with a bandage, but it still burned through the material. She glanced down at the gauze, noticing coarse, black hairs poking through the yellowing material.

Alice's head sank back into the pillow and she started clicking her tongue against the roof of her mouth. Soft, chittering noises.

Like a bug…

THE END